PEGGY PARSLEY

AND

THE BUZZY BUMBLES of HONEYCOMB COTTAGE

W. J. Bixby

ISBN, paperback: 978-1-80227-167-6
ISBN, ebook: 978-1-80227-168-3

For my husband Stuart
and children Victoria and Dean

Once upon a time, many years ago, there was a far richer land that was full of wild meadows and woodlands, where trees were left to grow tall and flourish. There was a wonderful sound of the wind whistling through the trees and rustling the rich leaves that grew on their enormous thick branches.

There were also glorious meadows filled with a vibrant blanket of colour as the wildflowers stretched for miles, providing much food for the bees to feed upon.

After saying goodbye to a dreary winter and hello to the much-welcomed signs of springtime, Mrs Bumble stirred sleepily from their warm cosy nest. The nests are made under the ground as this is where us bumblebees like to hibernate and keep warm until the cold dark winter months make way for the milder, brighter days of spring when all the shrubs start to awake and dance as the sun begins its work providing a gentle warmth on their delicate buds.

"Wakey, wakey, my little Bumbles," said **Mrs Bumble** softly, as she gently flapped the cobwebs from her restful wings and began fastening her pink apron around her waist. "Time to get up! Spring is here once again, and we have lots of chores to be done."

"That also includes you, **Mr Bumble**," she said firmly but with a warmth in her voice. She proceeded to hand Mr Bumble his favourite brown flat cap; Mr Bumble refused to go anywhere without it.

Bronte, Beatrice, Bobby, Benny and little baby Bluebell, all still sleepy, stirred in their nests. Yawning and stretching, they too shook the cobwebs from their young wings; apart from *baby Bluebell* as she was the youngest of the Bumble family and therefore still relied on the help of the other Bumbles!

Bronte was the eldest. She had big eyes and was always grooming her very long though quite beautiful eyelashes. She was the typical big sister; bossy but always had our best interests at heart.

Next is **Beatrice**; she was the quieter one, and had larger than average wings for a Bumble. I suppose you could say she had the wings of an angel but Beatrice was shy and always felt happier when she was with all her Bumble family, unlike the terrible twins, Bobby and Benny, who were always getting into mischief wherever they went.

We could only tell them apart by the spectacles that **Bobby** had to wear, unless **Benny** wore them to confuse us all when playing one of their many jokes on all of us!

Mr Bumble lifted **Bluebell** into his arms and gently blew the dust from her tiny wings. "Thank you, Daddy," said Bluebell in her sweet bumbling voice as she tried to flap her delicate wings by herself. "Oh, dear," said Bluebell in a sad tone. "When am I ever going to be able to use them properly?"

"Be patient, my little one," said Mr Bumble.
"All in good time!"

Mr Bumble carefully laid Bluebell back in her nest and proceeded to shake the dust off himself. While he was stretching, he let out the most enormous bumbling yawn. He beckoned to his children, meaning it was also time for them to get up and with that, Bronte, Beatrice, Bobby and Benny also let out a bumbling yawn as they too stretched and mimicked Mr Bumble's actions, which was something they always did, to Mr Bumble's amusement and great delight!

Mrs Bumble lifted baby Bluebell into her arms as Baby Bluebell was still far too young to fully shake her own wings and wash the sleep from her enormous brown eyes.

Mrs Bumble knew that Bluebell would have to stay at home for a little while longer... "But Mummy, why can't

I come with you?" buzzed Bluebell as she bumbled and stumbled, trying so very hard to fly and impress her mother. "I can see you're growing and getting stronger, my little Bluebell, but the world is a much harder place these days so I need you to be a little bigger and much stronger before you start on your adventures." "But Mummy," Bluebell pleaded. "Pleazzzze?" Bluebell buzzed. "No!" Mrs Bumble replied firmly. "No, Bluebell, and let that be the end of it." Bluebell shrugged her tiny wings and soon realised that her mother's words were final and there was no point trying to persuade her otherwise!

The Bumbles felt extremely fortunate to be living at Honeycomb Cottage. It rested amidst Bramble Common where wild daisies and buttercups are left to flourish and, once again, help provide plenty of nectar for the bumblebees and other insects to feed on.

Mrs Bumble emerged from her nest and caught the first sight of spring since the long winter nights of hibernation. "Oh," she gasped with much delight as she took a breath of the spring dawn air. The sun softly glistened on the morning dew and the air was so fresh and crisp as Mrs Bumble fluttered her strong wings.

As she flew gently around Honeycomb Cottage exploring the new buds of life beginning to blossom, she caught a glimpse of Ethel and Alfie Bixby. Such a dear sweet couple, thought Mrs Bumble to herself as she took time to nestle amongst the dewy shrubs and observe them pottering about their garden. Every year without fail, Ethel and Alfie would spend many hours of the day caring for their plants and growing such a colourful abundance of flowers and so Mrs Bumble knew there would be lots of nectar once again this year, just as every year before that, for us Bumbles to make into lots and lots of yummy honey!

Ethel was a dear sweet elderly lady, slightly rounded, with lovely silver hair, tied neatly in a bun. Her back was now slightly hunched and she had lovely twinkling blue eyes that crumpled at the corners when she smiled.

Alfie was a kind, quietly spoken man with thinning hair. His forehead was speckled with age spots but he remained as handsome as ever in Ethel's eyes.

Alfie and Ethel had been married for a good 50 years or more and had lived in Honeycomb Cottage since their wedding day. They had both worked and enjoyed their jobs very much. Alfie had worked as a groundsman for a large wealthy family, tending to their huge gardens, whilst Ethel had worked as a nurse in a local hospital. They first stumbled upon Honeycomb Cottage just by chance one day when they had decided to go exploring Bramble Common and had packed a picnic to make the most of the glorious sunshine.

"Oh, look!" squealed Ethel, shading her eyes with her hand from the midday sun. "Look, Alfie," Ethel said as she pointed across the common at the cottage in the distance.

As they got closer, they could see it was pretty tired and run-down with thistles and brambles roaming wild, covering the walls and pathways. Ethel opened the old rickety wooden gate, and as she did, it fell sideways,

catching her finger on a splinter. "Ouch!" said Ethel as she then caught her foot in a mass of overgrown nettles. As she turned, she noticed Alfie was trying hard not to laugh at her. Alfie reached out to her and gently took hold of her small delicate hand. Ethel was not put off by any means, and, with more determination than ever before, they both proceeded to ramble through the very unkempt garden.

"Look what I have found," said Alfie, and in his hand, he held an old wooden plaque. As he brushed away the cobwebs, it read Honeycomb Cottage. "Oh, Alfie," said Ethel, "what a wonderful name that is!" Ethel and Alfie made their way around the cottage trying to peer in as many windows as they possibly could. "Well," said Alfie, "it is definitely in need of some love and care." "Yes, absolutely," said Ethel, "and I don't think there is anyone else who could love this cottage as much as we could." With that, they looked into each other's eyes and knew, without saying any more that Honeycomb Cottage would be their forever home.

As the months followed, Ethel and Alfie worked hard, turning Honeycomb Cottage into a wonderful home full of love and joy.

Alfie worked hard tending the garden and planting an array of flowers to help all the bumblebees, butterflies and other insects they needed to be able to survive. Ethel and Alfie enjoyed observing the new buds of life starting to emerge and the gentle humming of the bumblebees. They watched closely as the bees immersed themselves and wiggled through the half-opened petals of the daffodils. It was at that moment they both realised what immense beauty was in nature and the importance of the wildlife that was all around them. At that moment, they knew that the garden would always be a safe and welcoming home for the bumbles. Yes, Honeycomb Cottage was indeed the perfect place to Beeeeee!

Ethel and Alfie had raised two wonderful children at Honeycomb Cottage, Peter and Gracie, who now have children of their own and Ethel and Alfie were so looking forward to their grandchild, Peggy, who was coming to stay for the summer holidays.

She is almost five now, with lovely soft ginger curls and eyes the colour of jade. Ethel said loudly, "I am so happy that Peggy is coming to stay with us for the summer holidays. It will be so wonderful to share our h o m e with our eldest grandchild!" Ethel's rosy cheeks were flushed with excitement. Alfie put his strong tanned arm around her shoulders and said, "Yes, my sweet Ethel, it will be a special time for all of us."

The weekend soon arrived and Ethel was fussing about the house, making sure everything was as it should be, neat and tidy. She had been up incredibly early, baking a jam and cream sponge cake for little Peggy and had spent ages preparing her bedroom. Her room had newly papered walls, covered in bright red poppies and tiny little figures of butterflies and bumblebees. Ethel patted the bed once more.

As she turned to leave, she caught a faint scent of heather that she had placed in a vase earlier that morning. As she turned to leave, she noticed a bumblebee nestling amongst the heather. "Hello, bumble, said Ethel. "What brings you inside on this lovely morning? My word," Ethel said gently, "you are just a baby yourself," and she carefully carried the tiny bumblebee and sprigs of heather outside to the garden so that the bumblebee could safely fly away.

Ethel carried the vase and heather back upstairs and once again placed them neatly by the window, allowing just enough breeze to cool the warm air.

As Ethel closed the bedroom door, she heard the car pull up on their drive.

"Alfie!" Ethel called excitedly. "Are they here?" "Yes, dear," he answered, sounding as thrilled as she was. Ethel ran down the stairs as fast as her worn legs could manage. She came flying out of the door just in time to see Alfie scoop little Peggy up in his arms and hear Peggy calling, "Grandpa! Grandpa, I have missed you so much!"

"Peggy!" Ethel called out. "My dear little Peggy Parsley," cried Ethel as she hugged her granddaughter tightly.

"Grandma, I am so happy to be having lots of sleeps here with you and Grandpa," said Peggy excitedly. "Oh

yes," replied Ethel, "my little Peggy Parsley. We are going to have such fun together."

Ethel took hold of Peggy's small hand and as they walked throw the door, Peggy said, "Oh Grandma, that is such a lovely smell!" as she inhaled the aroma deeply. "What are you making?" asked Peggy inquisitively. "A jam and cream sponge especially for you, my dear," replied Ethel lovingly. "Mmm, scrummy," replied Peggy as she tossed her tousled curls back from her rosy cheeks.

"Would you like to go and see your bedroom now?" suggested Ethel, all excited to show her granddaughter her bedroom. "Oh, yes please, Grandma Ethel," replied Peggy excitedly as she turned and ran speedily up the wooden staircase.

As Peggy opened the bedroom door, she gasped and with eyes wider than saucers, said, "Oh my, Grandma, it is so beautiful!" Peggy ran her little hands over the wallpaper.

"Poppies, Grandma, poppies, bumbles and butterflies. My favourites. I am going to enjoy all my sleeps here, Grandma," said Peggy as she threw herself on the soft bed and, with dreamy eyes, nodded off into a restful sleep.

Ethel placed a blanket carefully over Peggy's tiny frame and gently kissed the soft curls resting on her forehead.

Closing the bedroom door, Ethel quietly tiptoed down the wooden staircase.

"Peggy is fast asleep," Ethel said to Alfie. "She must have been so exhausted after such a long drive."

"Yes, my dear," replied Alfie, "a sleep will do her the world of good."

And with that, Ethel attended to her baking whilst Alfie once again pottered about the garden.

Peggy woke to the smell of the heather as the warm and gentle breeze blew softly through the window. As she stretched and gave out a huge yawn, she heard the weirdest sound.

"Who is there?" said Peggy as she quietly tiptoed over to the window.

"Bzzzzzz," it went again.

"Hello," said Peggy as she saw the loveliest and tiniest bumblebee but with the most enormous beautiful brown eyes, nestling among the sweet-smelling heather.

"Bzzzzzzzz bzzzzzzz."

"My name is Peggy," she said as her eyes studied the bumblebee with curiosity.

"Bluebell BZZZZZZZZ."

Peggy's eyes widened with amazement.

"You can talk!" said Peggy in astonishment.

"Yezzzzzzzz," buzzed Bluebell. "Yezzzz, I can indeed."

"This is sooo amazzzzing," replied Peggy, giggling that she too was beginning to make buzzing sounds just like the bumblebee.

Peggy started telling her new friend Bluebell all about her staying for many sleeps at her Grandma and Grandpa Bixby's and how excited she was about stopping in the countryside as Peggy's house back home was surrounded by lots and lots of tall buildings and the roads were filled with noisy cars and lorries and not as safe when riding a bike.

"Oh dear," said Peggy, thinking out loud. "I do hope Mummy remembered to get my bike from the trunk as I have been so looking forward to riding my bike

at Honeycomb Cottage!" And fortunately, her mother had not forgotten to pack her bike. "Oh," said Bluebell as she admired the bright blue bike and shiny bell. "All aboard!" said Peggy giggling......

And so, the adventure began as Peggy and Bluebell went off together down the quiet lane with Bluebell holding on tightly to Peggy's curls.

"Ph, Puh," Blue Bell spluttered as her tiny wings became entangled in Peggy's tight curls.

"Bzzzzzzz," said Bluebell. "Bzzzzzzzzz."

Peggy giggled as she pedalled tirelessly through the lane, feeling carefree and so happy that she had found such a wonderful yet vastly different friend who just happened to be a bumblebee!

Peggy and Bluebell became inseparable over the coming days. They sat in the meadows chatting merrily and learning so much about each other.

Peggy learnt about Bluebell's family and that because she was still a baby Bumble, she had to stay at home while the other Bumbles went out to find nectar from all the flowers and shrubs and were always especially thankful for all the wonderful flowers Peggy's grandparents so kindly provided every year!

Bluebell learnt all about Peggy's house and the busy built-up streets where there were not too many gardens and parks, which Bluebell thought was incredibly sad for all the other bumblebees in the world!

One day, as Peggy was sat in the glorious meadow, eating from the picnic that her sweet Grandma Ethel had packed so neatly, Bluebell decided to fly off in search of her own picnic. As she flapped her tiny delicate wings, buzzing from one wildflower to another, she soon realised how tired and exhausted she was becoming. Bluebell

decided she should rest a while and nestled amongst the long corn for a much-needed sleep!

"Oh dear," said Peggy, anxiously calling Bluebell's name over and over. "Where are you, Bluebell? Grandma and Grandpa will start to worry so we really must be getting back."

Peggy listened intently but could not hear even a faint buzz from Bluebell, so, reluctantly, she sadly packed away her picnic basket and headed back to Honeycomb Cottage all alone.

As Peggy watched the sun setting from her bedroom window and the birds returning to their nests for the night, she patiently waited for the safe return and the lovely buzz of her dear friend Bluebell. But as night fell, there was no sign of her. Peggy rubbed the tears from her swollen eyes and fell into a restless sleep.

A new day soon dawned. Peggy awoke and all the memories of the day before engulfed her. She jumped from her warm bed and ran over to the heather her Grandma had placed by the window, but sadly, there was still no sign of Bluebell. Peggy shrugged her small shoulders wearily and then thought to herself, 'I must go back to the meadows and search for Bluebell!'

Peggy quickly washed and dressed herself and sped through the lane, pedalling her bike as fast as her little legs would go!

Peggy searched and searched.

"Bluebell!" she called out tirelessly and repeatedly!

Peggy sat wearily in the meadows and as she laid her head down to take a much-needed rest, she noticed hovering above her were two of the most beautiful butterflies she had ever seen. They were a deep shade of white that glistened like gold dust as the sun shone on their delicate wings.

"Oh my," said Peggy as they gently fluttered and laid something very small in her hand. 'Am I dreaming?' thought Peggy to herself as she saw this tiny, somewhat lifeless bumblebee.

"Oh Bluebell!" Peggy cried out.

Bluebell lay almost lifeless in Peggy's small hand. She desperately tried to flap her wings but was far too weak.

"My poor Bluebell!" Peggy cried. "Whatever has happened to you? Let me get you back safely home to Honeycomb Cottage!"

Peggy wrapped little Bluebell in her handkerchief and carefully placed her inside her pocket and once again pedalled back to Honeycomb Cottage as fast as her legs would go. "Oh, my dear Peggy, whatever is the matter?" said Grandma Ethel. "Oh, Grandma, Grandpa!" Peggy sobbed, wiping the tears from her swollen red eyes. "It's, it's, oh ...." "Come inside," said Grandma, putting her arms around Peggy's quivering shoulders.

"You sit down there, and Grandma will make you a nice mug of hot milk."

Peggy sat down as Grandma had asked and carefully took the handkerchief from her pocket, placing it gently down on the kitchen table.

"There, there, my dear little Peggy," said Ethel. "Drink up and tell your Grandma what has upset you so."

Peggy looked down at the handkerchief and, pointing to it, Peggy said, "It's Bluebell, Grandma."

"Bluebell?" replied Ethel.

"Yes, Grandma, Bluebell. She is my friend."

Peggy went on to explain how she had come to know her new friend and how much fun they had had together since Peggy came to visit.

"And now she is .... Oh, Grandma," sobbed Peggy.

Ethel picked up the mug of warm milk and placed it in Peggy's small hands.

"Drink up, my dear," said Ethel in a soft voice.

Alfie stood in the doorway listening intently to Peggy's sadness over her friend Bluebell.

"So, who have we here?" asked Alfie.

Peggy looked up into her grandpa's kind eyes.

"It's little Bluebell, Grandpa. I think she may be.... I think she is..." Peggy's shoulders began to shudder once again. Alfie sat himself on a chair next to Peggy and as he placed his strong comforting arm around her, he said, "I think it would be best for Bluebell if we take a peek and see how she's doing, don't you think so?"

Peggy sat there twiddling the ends of her cardigan and as she wiped the tears from her flushed pink cheeks, she once again looked up into her grandpa's eyes and said, "Yes, I think we should."

With Grandpa Alfie and Grandma Ethel by her side, Peggy felt safe and very slowly she began to unfold the handkerchief... They all watched and waited in much anticipation as this tiny little Bumble lay very still amid the crumpled hanky.

"Buzz... bzzzzz."

"Did you hear that?" said Peggy, moving her ear closer to Bluebell, but Alfie and Ethel's hearing wasn't as good as it once was.

"Bzzzzzz," it went again and with that, Bluebell wiggled her tiny wings.

"Oh, look!" cried Peggy. "Did you see that? She is going to be ok, isn't she?" asked Peggy.

Alfie and Ethel glanced over at each other and seeing their little granddaughter's joyful expression, they both realized that little Bluebell was not quite out of the woods yet.

Now Alfie and Ethel knew only too well the importance of bumblebees and the love and care needed to keep them safe when visiting your garden. Grandpa fetched a small matchbox from the fireplace.

"We will make this Bluebell's bed for now," said Alfie and with that, Peggy very gently placed Bluebell inside the matchbox, talking to her softly and reassuring her that she was soon going to feel much better.

Grandma brought in a small shallow dish.

"What is that for?" asked Peggy inquisitively.

"Oh, this is water with a little sugar," said Grandma Ethel. "Bumbles need this to keep their strength up when they are poorly."

Bluebell, though very weak, struggled to sit up but Grandma Ethel held a teaspoonful of water for little Bluebell who was able to take a tiny sip.

"Can Bluebell sleep in my bedroom tonight?" asked Peggy.

"I do not see why not," said Grandma Ethel, looking at the sadness in her granddaughter's eyes.

Peggy carefully carried Bluebell up the wooden staircase and placed her little matchbox bed on her bedside table with the bowl of sugary water as it was especially important that Bluebell stayed hydrated. Bluebell had, once again, fallen asleep.

"Sleep tight, my little Bluebell," Peggy said, and with that, she quietly closed the bedroom door leaving Bluebell to rest.

Peggy did not have much of an appetite that evening as she sat around the table with her grandparents, pushing her fork around her plate and resting her head on her other hand.

"Try and eat up, Peggy," said Grandma Ethel.

"You need to keep your strength up if you want to take care of Bluebell."

"Ok, Grandma," replied Peggy as she slowly ate her supper.

After supper, Peggy had her normal daily bath and put on her freshly ironed pyjamas ready for bedtime. This was then followed by a bedtime story read by Grandpa Alfie. As Peggy climbed onto Grandpa Alfie's lap, she snuggled herself into his chest.

"Grandpa, where is my story book?" Peggy asked.

"I am not going to read that story this evening, my little Peggy Parsley. I am going to tell you a story about the bumblebees of Honeycomb Cottage. Once upon a time...." Grandpa said and told Peggy all about the Bumble family that lived in a hole in Honeycomb Cottage's garden and how important it was to provide flowers to help feed them.

"So, if the flowers and bugs are so good for them, why is Bluebell so poorly?" she asked.

"Well, my little Peggy, I think it may be because Bluebell has eaten something that was poisonous," replied Grandpa.

"Like what?" asked Peggy, curious, her eyes now as big as saucers.

"Pesticides," replied Grandpa.

"Pesticides?" quizzed Peggy.

"Yes, sometimes people and farmers put this on their fields and gardens to help the growth, but it can be very harmful to the bumblebees and other wildlife. And I think that maybe this is very likely why Bluebell is so unwell."

"Oh, my poor Bluebell!" replied Peggy as tears began to well up again in her sad eyes.

"But she will be alright, Grandpa, won't she?"

"We can only wait and hope," replied Grandpa Alfie reassuringly.

Peggy kissed her grandpa softly on the cheek and, saying good night, she headed up to bed. "Here is a warm mug of milk for you," said Grandma Ethel. "Drink up, my dear. It will help you to sleep." "Thank you, Grandma," replied Peggy and then they both quietly leant over and blew a kiss to a sound asleep and poorly Bluebell.

Peggy was awoken by a faint buzzing sound, and, rubbing the sleep from her eyes, she gasped to see bumblebees gently flying above her head.

"Bzzzzzz! Bzzzzzzzz!"

Peggy could not count very well as she was only just five but she knew there were more than four bees. As Peggy lay there watching in astonishment, little Bluebell landed right on the tip of Peggy's nose.

"Oh, Bluebell!" said Peggy with such excitement. "Yes," Bluebell replied. "It is me and thanks to your care, I am feeling much better."

The other bees gathered round, and Bluebell introduced her dear friend Peggy to all the Bumble family. "This is my wonderful family!" said Bluebell.

"This is Mr Bumble, Mrs Bumble and Bronte, Beatrice, Bobby and Benny."

"Thank you so much for taking care of our Bluebell," said Mr and Mrs Bumble.

"Yes, thank you," said all the Bumbles, "for getting Bluebell safely back to all of us!"

They were all excitedly flapping their wings. As you can guess, Bluebell got a telling off from Mr and Mrs Bumble for disobeying them, but they were just so happy that Bluebell had returned home safely at last.

Peggy was invited to the Bumble's home for supper, so later that day, she followed them to the end of the garden where Peggy saw an extremely small hole just beneath the old birch tree. "How on earth can I fit down there?" said Peggy in bemusement. Bluebell perched herself once again on the tip of Peggy's nose, and looking deep into Peggy's eyes, she said, "All you need to do is wish.

Close your eyes and make a wish."

"A wish?" replied Peggy.

"Yes, a wish," said Bluebell. "Make a wish to be tiny like us and let your imagination do the rest."

With that, Peggy closed her eyes and wished that she could be as small as a Bumble.

"Open your eyes!" the Bumbles all said excitedly. Peggy squinted and slowly opened one eye, then the other, and to her amazement, she was in the Bumble's house!

"Oh my!" gasped Peggy as she pinched herself to see if she was real. "Oh, how you have all grown!" squealed Peggy with delight as the Bumbles were as big as she.

"No, not us, my dear," replied Mrs Bumble. "It is you who is as small as we."

And they all began laughing and buzzzzzzzing together!

Peggy sat comfortably around the wooden table eating honey and chatting merrily with all the Buzzy Bumbles, learning about how important it is to look after our bees and not to be afraid of them as they will not sting you unless you try to hurt them.

"Peggy... Peggy. Wake up, my dear. It is a beautiful day and I have made you some pancakes with lots of honey."

Once again, Peggy rubbed her sleepy eyes, slipped on her cosy pink slippers and headed down the wooden stairs for breakfast. 'Oh, not more honey,' thought Peggy quietly giggling to herself.

"Good morning, Peggy Parsley," said Grandpa Alfie. "I hope you have slept well."

"Yes, thank you, Grandpa. I am so happy that Bluebell is much better, and I went and had supper at the Bumble's too.

"Bluebell?" replied Grandpa inquisitively.

"Oh, Grandpa," replied Peggy with a giggle. "Yes, my friend Bluebell that you and Grandma helped last night. The bumblebee...."

Grandma Ethel, placing the warm pancakes in front of Peggy, glanced curiously across the table towards Alfie.

"Peggy, my dear," said Grandpa Alfie. "I do believe you must have *been* dreaming!"

"No, Grandpa, it was not a dream. It was very real, and I went into their house and had supper and lots of honey with all the Bumble family."

"My, my," said Grandma Ethel, gently resting her hand on Peggy's shoulder. "But it is True!" said Peggy, Annoyed. "I did; truly I did..."

"Sometimes," said Grandpa Alfie, "we have dreams that can feel very real."

"And sometimes," said Grandma, "we can have dreams that are wonderful just like yours has been."

Peggy scuffed her feet, and pulling a sulky face, walked off into the garden. Feeling the warm morning sunshine on her face, she ventured over to the old birch tree and there it was - the same small hole as she had seen in her dreams!

Peggy stood there and closed her eyes, wishing as hard as she possibly could that she would be as small as a bumblebee. She opened her eyes and with much disappointment, found herself still stood under the old tree. Just before she had time to feel the tears begin to well up in her eyes...

"Bzzzzzzz, Bzzzzzzz,"

Bluebell landed once again on the tip of Peggy's nose.

"Bluebell!" squealed Peggy excitedly. "You really are real! I knew it, I truly did."

"Oh yes, we are truly real, my dear friend," replied Bluebell, "but it will have to be our secret so you must never, never tell a living soul. You have a gift and are able to talk to all animals. You must use it wisely, to help and teach others to take care of all the wildlife as you have helped me, my little Peggy Parsley. But remember, your wishes will only come true when you go to sleep and then your dreams and imagination will take you to the most wonderful magical places and many more adventures with the Bumbles of Honeycomb Cottage. And Friends......."

ACKNOWLEDGEMENTS

I would like to thank my two wonderful children, my daughter Victoria and my son Dean, for their constant love and support. Also, thanks to my wonderful husband Stuart for the selfless love and encouragement he has given me.

However long it may take, it's never too late to chase your dreams.

From every seed a flower grows, a pot or window box, will do, water well and watch it bloom and soon the bumbles will come to you.

"Be patient, my little one," said Mr Bumble.
"All in good time!"

"Oh, dear," said Bluebell in a sad tone. "When am I ever going to be able to use them properly?"

Lightning Source UK Ltd.
Milton Keynes UK
UKHW050824170821
388975UK00002B/116